Lafayette Hotel
101 Front Street
Marietta, OH 45750
39.410726, -81.452461

Ghosts Inside the Hotel

The beginning of Marietta called the Picketed Point Stockade was completed in 1791. The mouth of the Muskingum is to the left. The Ohio River is in forefront. It is along West Ohio Street—early on around 1788, there was a tavern built where the Bellevue Hotel was built and after, the Lafayette Hotel.

In 1786, men from Massachusetts formed a real estate company and called themselves the Ohio Company of Associates. They set their sights on the purchase of a massive chunk of property in the Northwest Territory that, at the time, was a vast, untamed land of wilderness.

They were successful in their endeavors. To promote settlement, Congress offered even more land to the company that would be free for colonists and function as a buffer between the white settlements and Indians. In return for this land, the company was also required to set aside property for education, government, and religion, along with two townships with a university.

The first settlement was established along the Ohio River at the junction with the Muskingum River. It was called Adelphia, and its name would later be changed to Marietta, christened so for the French Queen Marie Antoinette. A fortification was built along with homes, a school, and a church. The community would thrive, becoming a hub of activity along the river as a trading center with a multitude of manufacturing businesses.

The lay of the land and the buildings would change over time, including one prime piece of real estate—the riverfront point where the Ohio and Muskingum rivers meet and where boats would dock full of travelers. There in 1892, the elegant four-story Bellevue Hotel was built. It offered fifty-five steam-heated rooms at the cost of $2.00 or $3.00 per room per night, a call bell system in each room, and hot/cold baths. It even had its own bar.

The Bellevue Hotel—

Table of Contents

Catastrophe struck on April 26, 1916, when the Bellevue was engulfed in flames after an accidental fire in a storage room on the top floor. It was rebuilt and opened its doors to travelers again on July 1, 1918.

Bellevue burned on April 26, 1916. Many guests were dining and were able to run to their rooms to retrieve their belongings. The fourth floor was completely gutted along with most of the furniture. *Image: Bellevue Hotel ablaze via S. Durward Hoag Collection, Marietta College Legacy Library Special Collections*

It was renamed the Lafayette Hotel for the Frenchman Marquis de Lafayette, a close friend and ally of General Washington during the American Revolution. Lafayette made a surprise visit to the city in 1825, close to the present-day location of the hotel. He was admired for volunteering his time and money to help the American cause.

It is in the infancy of the hotel where the man who is said to haunt the Lafayette makes his worldly appearance. Stephen Hoag was only eighteen in 1918 when he first started working at the hotel his father first managed and later owned. He was employed as assistant manager/vice president before entering a partnership with his father as owners and managers.

Above: Mister Hoag, previous owner of The Lafayette. The Lafayette Hotel.

After his father's death, Stephen continued to operate the hotel. He retired and sold the Lafayette in 1973 and died on November 19, 1995. He was considered 'larger than life,' a man ambitious enough to get the government to shift the plans for Interstate 77 so that it crossed the Ohio River bridge to Marietta. Stephen Hoag was a go-getter with a vision for his city and he expanded the hotel continuously. He was an avid photographer and travel writer for the town. It would seem fitting the man who had ties to the hotel for over fifty-five years and who had helped build a tourism industry in the city can be seen on the third floor occasionally, still putting on a show for the visitors who accompany the guides on the popular ghost tours given in town.

Workers at the hotel have witnessed strange, quick bursts of light, something akin to the flicker of a camera flash. Not surprising as Mister Hoag was well known in the community as a photographer. Visitors to the hotel have felt the presence of an older man, a shadowy figure, wandering the halls of the third floor where Mister Hoag lived. Some have seen Mister Hoag sitting in the far corner of the dining area, a well-dressed man deep in thought who vanishes suddenly.

I had a friend who would visit Lafayette quite often. He said it relaxed him there more than any other place. He also liked the older woman who wandered the hotel, although the first time he met her, he watched her make her slow walk down the third floor hallway toward him. He addressed her with his usual friendly smile and greeting, thinking she was just another guest. And she disappeared!

The third floor of the hotel where the presence of Mister Hoag is heard and felt. An aged woman has also been seen wandering around.

One of the front desk agents for the Lafayette stated that although the employees do not regularly get glimpses of the ghost, visitors often notify the staff about strange occurrences. Quite often, guests find furniture moved in the rooms. And there have even been occurrences where chairs are placed in front of the doors. At times, people are overwhelmed by icy cold spots while walking the hallways.

The elevator has a funny life of its own, a ghostly finger pushing buttons—it has been known to travel all by itself at night, up and down the floors.

A little boy ghost has been seen hanging around outside the women's bathrooms.

And then, there is the little ghost boy in the clothing of the late 1800s who stands by the door of the women's restroom on the bottom floor. No one is sure why he is there, hanging out for a moment before he disappears.

Levee House
127 Ohio Street
Marietta, OH 45750
39.411120, -81.449810

Legend of the Hatchet Killer

The Levee House has been used along the riverfront since 1826 (3-story building to left) with a wide variety of uses including a saloon and ill-famed boarding house.

Drawn to the growing trade possibilities along the Ohio River at the Ohio Company's main settlement at Marietta, Dudley Woodbridge became the proprietor of the first mercantile in Marietta in 1788. His dry goods business was later passed on to his son, Dudley Woodbridge Jr, who was well known for being both "strong in his opinions, but also in his prejudices."

Around 1826, a three-story brick structure was built along the waterfront and set up as a mercantile—what is now called the Levee House.

It would be the first dry goods store in the Northwest Territory. As his business grew, Dudley Jr. moved to larger quarters. Many times, the building would change hands, becoming Braddock Liquor Store, a boarding house/bordello, hotels—The La Belle, and then Golden Eagle that purportedly had pubs below and brothels in the rooms above and a saloon owned by Peter Klein. When Prohibition rolled around, the doors were locked to liquor sales. Over time, it was an assembly area for Studebakers, a car repair shop, and the Levee House Café.

This building on Ohio Street has been many different things to many different people over the years, each giving it a personality of its own. There was a time during the 1890s oil boom that this particular part of town was overrun with saloons and brothels. Thus, the owners and the building fell into disrepute.

Many raids were made by Marietta police for drunken brawls and prostitution on this now quiet street. *Marietta Daily Leader—May 16, 1898.*

ANOTHER RAID.

Eight Abandoned Women Locked up by the Police Saturday Night.

The police made another raid on the disreputable houses Saturday night. Two places on Ohio street, one kept by Mary Snyder and the other by George Tittle, were pulled and eight women were locked up. We are informed that several men were in one of the houses at the time of the raid, but were allowed to go. The women will have a hearing before Mayor Richardson today.

It is no surprise that ghostly legends have cropped up around this building. The Levee House story came from the period when its downstairs was a saloon, and the upstairs was a boarding house for prostitutes. One local wealthy man would slip up the back alleys and slide into the front doors during this time. He would partake of the drink offered at the saloon, then sneak upstairs to visit one of the women.

That is, until one night when his son watched him leave home. Curious of the gossip that had caught his ears of his father's clandestine affairs and feeling humiliated by it, the young man followed the older man down the dark streets and to the front door of the La Belle. The closer he got to the river, the shabbier the houses became. The road was muddy, gritty, and dirty here, with puddles of horse manure left unheeded. He listened to the drunken laughter and revelry riding the air along the river. There were angry shouts and chatter. Dogs barked far off, and a couple of stray, mangy cats skulked around the building.

It was the roughest part of town. Shadows milled about the buildings, the dark silhouettes of those up to no good. The young man knew what went on inside the building where his father had stepped inside—the wild drinking, the sordid women. The young man must have waited outside for some time as the anger built, pacing along the walkway with the dirt path crunching beneath his feet. Then, when he could stand it no longer, he crept through the tavern with eyes peering wildly about for his father, who was not in sight. He mixed with the guests before working his way up the dark staircase until he heard the deep voice he recognized as his father's. The man stepped to the door, slowly and cautiously, and when he wiggled the knob and pushed the entry open, his father was there along with one of the prostitutes.

There lay a hatchet for chopping the firewood to finer pieces by the fireplace. Crazy with anger, the son lunged forward and snatched up the hatchet. Then, he let the blade fall hard upon his father's skull. As the man fell, the prostitute screeched, and the blood spurted out of the older man's head, flowing to the floor. The son realized what he had done in his fury, and fear gripped him so hard he was dizzy with regret and fright. He shoved the door open, bounding with heavy steps down the stairway, and fled into the night.

The Levee House today along the riverfront where ghostly steps of a young man's murderous flight are heard.

The man died, and the son was apprehended. He was acquitted after a lengthy court battle because the murder was committed in "a crime of passion." Now, those near enough to the building to hear can catch the faint trample of feet on the stairway and heavy, heart-pounding breaths—a phantom flight of a young man still grasping the hatchet that killed his father and also clinging, perhaps, to regret.

Buckley Island
(AKA Kerrs Island, Crescent, Duvalls Island, Meigs Island)
Buckley Island
Williams, WV 26187
39.408541, -81.445400

View from Marietta:
Ohio Riverfront Park
201 Ohio Street
Marietta, OH 45750
39.410638, -81.449927

The Many Faces of an Island.
And the Ghosts that Come with it.

Buckley Island has been known by many names throughout history—including Kerrs Island, Duvalls Island, and Meigs Island. It also has a few ghosts. Pictures belie its length—2.6 miles long!

Those who walk the shoreline and boat along the Ohio River have heard ghostly cries and voices coming from an island near Marietta. Sometimes they see shadows lurking around the water's edge. This 160-acre island is technically in West Virginia but is mostly associated with Marietta and has, in the past, been called Marietta Island. Along its 2.6-mile length, it has so much history; it is difficult to point the finger at who is attached to these phantom voices and sounds—

In the 1780s, a flatboat was working south along the river. The waters could be rough there seasonally, and the wind quite brutal blowing along the river valley. It could be almost impossible to see the path ahead when fog would slide in, especially the dark island blending with the mist and brown, muddy water.

One boat heading toward New Orleans ran into that fog in 1782, and the steersman could not wheel the ship fast enough, right or left, so the vessel wrecked at the head of the island. The travelers camped there for the night while the boat was repaired. Sometime during that night, a band of Indians hunting on the island came upon the stranded travelers. They murdered two men and captured the rest. Could it be their cries heard riding the wind?

Across from Marietta (left) was Fort Harmar, built in 1785, as a buffer between the Indian and the settler territories. From the view, it appears early in Marietta's settlement in 1788. In the background is Buckley Island where many travelers would pass from the 1700s onward on their way along the river. *Image: Mrs. L. A. Alderman E.R. Alderman & Sons, printers, 1887 - Marietta*

Or the sounds could have been from its early years when smallpox took a holiday in Marietta. It started in 1790, in one of the coldest of months—January. A boat heading for Kentucky docked in Marietta, carrying a sick passenger with a fever and headache.

Ready to come to the traveler's aid, the James and Mary Owen family took the man into their home and provided a bed for him to heal. When the bubbled rash and fluid-filled pustules appeared on the man's face and body, they were thunderstruck to find out he had the dreaded and contagious smallpox. Quickly, the town organized to build a quarantine hospital or pest house away from the city to stop the spread. Workers constructed the building near the area where Marietta College stands now. The poor traveler was whisked away to the hospital but did not recover. Mary Owen came down with the sickness, but she lived.

Fearing the worst, those within the town decided to take the risk of using an early form of vaccination by inoculating healthy people by a simple scratch on the skin with matter from one of the sores of the sick. Pest houses were built around the town to tend to the ill, with two doctors attending them. Of the over one-hundred people vaccinated, only two died.

Three years later, scarlet fever and smallpox spread throughout Picketed Point, aided by the close quarters of militia soldiers living there. During this time, a pest house was added to an island that John Pierce Duvall had used to raise corn in the 1770s, such its name— Duvalls Island. It would later be known as Buckley Island. Its access was easier then because, before the locks and dam, the water between the land and the island was not deep. In the summer, folks could wade across to the island. In the winter, the water froze to a hard sheen of easily traversed ice. It is the sick and dying who used the pest house on the island calling out for some recourse from the horrible deaths.

Or it could be a young man who was sent over to the island for milk when Hamilton Kerr, an Indian fighter, had a small cabin on it around 1787. The young man never returned alive. He was scalped and killed somewhere between.

A towboat glides past this island with a ghostly past.

But the river has also taken in many drowned souls on its own whose spirits may be out there wandering around aimlessly looking for a home. The body of 17-year-old Robert Waters, a tool dresser, who had drowned upriver from Marietta on June 28, 1896, washed ashore at the wharf after rolling around in the waters for three days. He had been bantering around with three of his friends in a skiff on the river. A fourth jumped in, tossing the other three out. Waters was pulled under and could not swim back to the boat. The Marietta Daily Leader expressed, "the body was considerably disfigured by having rolled on the bottom of the river and was not a pleasant sight" to those who found him.

On a windy Saturday, June 25, 1898, the United Commercial Travelers Company had engaged the steamer Wm. Duffy for an excursion to Buckeye Park, an amusement park built on Buckley Island by Buckeye and Eureka Pipeline Company. The boat was filled with two-hundred eager travelers for one final tour to the island. It left the wharf and was close to the banks when suddenly a gust burst up the river. That wind toppled a derrick used to anchor wires supporting the Buckeye Pipe Line as it crossed the river.

The cables were dipping almost into the river. Fearing the boat would be tangled in them, the captain veered heartily toward the island, and the boat dipped dangerously close to the water. At the same time, passengers were rushing to that side to flee an unexpected downpour of rain. Another blast of wind hit the high side of the boat, sending it keeling even farther into the river, where it took on water. As it capsized, some were able to scramble to the deck, but others were tossed into the river before the boat righted itself. Many were saved, but three men died in the accident—including Malcolm Nye—a 24-year-old graduate of Marietta Academy, whose career had just begun. Their bodies were recovered, but some believe the spirits of the dead remain. Passersby hear screams on windy days over the rattle of tree leaves.

The island with many names and many ghosts.

In early April of 1930, 29-year-old George Davis and 17-year-old Silbert Smith sailed near Buckley Island, riding the cold water while the spring breezes patted their sails. Suddenly an unexpected gust of wind blew in, and the boat toppled to its side, spilling out the two men who were swept into the dam below and lost.

They have not been the only ones to drown here. On August 9, 1921, 13-year-old Arthur McFadden fell from the dam near the island, his body consumed in the depths. In June of 1964, a couple in a motorboat towing a skier drowned when their boat went over the dam.

It is less frightening to think that the phantom sounds heard over the water are the residual happy sounds of the employees and their families from Eureka Pipeline Company. From 1897 to 1906, the company made an amusement park and picnicking area for their employees on the island. But we may never know whose voices are calling out, shouting, screaming, or laughing. There are just far too many who have died in the depths of the Ohio River. Although the island has been a haven for most travelers along the water, it has not been for all. So next time you are walking along the shores, stop and listen carefully, and you can make out some words, some message from those dead to let us know their identity.

But be careful while you listen. Do not get too caught up trying to follow the calls that you step into the water yourself, skid on the slippery moss, and get sucked into the river. It might be a trick, a siren-like creature luring you in just like the rest who have died there, who have been killed, murdered, or drowned.

St. Cloud Hotel
190—194 Front Street
Marietta, OH 45750
39.412678, -81.453492

Lurking and Lingering on Front Street

St Cloud Hotel in its heyday—decorated for Marietta centennial April 7, 1888. Where it stood is now a parking lot. *Picture: Washington County Public Library*

St. Cloud Hotel was built upon a property with a history of lodging even before being established as one of Marietta's finest hotels. It was the Union House, a hotel run by Frederick and Elizabeth Gross.

The St. Cloud had a full life with more than just the appearance of a hotel under its belt. In the late 1930s, a fire from a stovepipe swept through the fourth floor. Most of the building suffered grave damage, but it was renovated with steam heat installed. Before it burned down in March of 2010, it was home to Goodwill and the Marietta Wine Cellars.

St. Cloud Hotel (left) —1890s. *Image: Marietta College Special Collections*

Where this iconic building once stood and accommodated thousands of travelers, and later shoppers is now a parking lot. All that remains are a few ghosts from its past, along with a dark figure that has found its place among the long-dead in this town who have lingered far too long after death. It remains near the curb, and when it disappears, a strange, guttural grunt lingers before fading away.

The building had a long life as a hotel, but like all the properties close to the Ohio River and along Front Street, seasonally, it was prone to being partially underwater. Midway through March of 1898, torrential rain and storms inundated Ohio. By Wednesday, March 23rd, everyone along the river was standing anxiously, watching as the Ohio River rose at four inches per hour and continued rising at this rate through Thursday.

It had passed the banks, then the sidewalks and streets, before less-than-reluctantly trespassed into homes and businesses. On Friday, when it settled on just a couple inches per hour, church bells rang out along with whistles, whoops, and hollers. They came from those now relieved but who had been panicking that another full-fledged flood would rage through the city as it had so heartily fourteen years earlier in 1884 when the height of overflow was almost fifty-three feet.

St Cloud during flooding-note the ornate balcony still intact. And the person standing atop it. *Picture: Washington County Public Library*

Over at the St. Cloud Hotel, an assembly of thirteen men had collected themselves on a flimsy iron balcony to watch the water flow through the street below. At best, their perch was precarious; they had entered utilizing an open window as no door opened to this faux balcony. The terrace was for ornate purposes and not built to withhold any weight. The only support was by street-level awning posts made of light iron.

Front Street during early flooding. *Picture: Washington County Public Library*

The balcony gave way with the weight, and the men tossed into the eight feet of surging water. One by one, each was able to swim to safety or were pulled by rescuers from the savage, swirling water. However, one man was missed immediately—cheerful, 52-year-old George Hudson—a senior member of Hudson and Riggs Undertaking had not surfaced. Knowing the body was undoubtedly caught beneath the balcony wreckage, James Whiting made heroic dive after dive until he located the body wedged beneath the iron poles. A rope was attached to the debris, and the balcony heaved sufficiently upward to release the man. Too late, though, George Hudson was dead.

The dark shadow seen where the building once stood is one of the thousands of visitors who used it as a hotel or store just going about their afterlife, utterly oblivious that they are dead. But I cannot help but wonder if it is not the undertaker who got smooshed beneath the balcony during the flood, reliving the last moments of his life—forever.

Where the St. Cloud Hotel stood is now the St. Cloud Parking Lot and perhaps, the home to a ghost or two.

Hackett Hotel/The Galley
203 2nd Street
Marietta, OH 45750
39.413563, -81.453637

Flickering Lights and Crashing Bottles

The Hackett Hotel and The Galley Restaurant.

There was an open sewage system running through Marietta in the late 1800s, where all the downtown buildings with outhouses drained right into nearby Goose Run and its basin. Not only was the sewer an eyesore and health hazard, but there seemed to be unique problems arising for each of the seasons as the years progressed and especially in the heat of summer.

The city planned to rid the unhealthy open system and build a new, brick sewer system below ground, but they knew the cost would be high. Then with funds and materials from the railway station located only across the road who were looking for more room for their railyard, Colonel John H. Riley solved the problem and found a way to reclaim the land. He covered the drainage area and, in 1899, built the three-floor Hackett Hotel right on top.

The hotel was a popular stopping place close to the train station and railyards. It offered bowling and even a bar. But as years passed, the hotel fell into disrepair until it got a new lease on life as The Galley. Above, it is now a renovated 5-room hotel with the aura of the past, 20th-century décor, and modern conveniences. On the lower floor is a restaurant and The Adelphia Music Hall.

Along with the renovations, people began noticing strange phenomena—the flickering of lights, the feeling someone is standing in the dark corner of a room when no one is there. There is the spirit of a woman who focuses on the males who enter the building. When men are around, there seems to be more slamming of doors and tables moving on their own. Bottles and glasses are swept off the bar and sent flying to the floor. The Hackett Hotel and The Galley get 5-star ratings. Guests say they like it because of its proximity to entertainment and the rooms are classy, and the beds are super comfortable. If well-decorated and charming are what you are looking for, along with the modern conveniences like wi-fi, you have picked the right place—just make sure you leave room for the ghosts!

Tiber Way—Sanitorium
8 Tiber Way
Marietta, OH 45750
39.413286, -81.453231

**Pampering Services for the Living
and the Dead**

Tiber Way—once Marietta's sanitorium—note the ghost
advertising on the top of the building: CHRONIC DISEASES.

A second structure built by Colonel John H. Riley
next to the Hackett Hotel was also used to help rid the
community of the sewer eyesore—a sanitorium, a
hospital for long-term illness such as tuberculosis.
These hospitals provided rest and fresh air and, in
many cases, massage and specialized hot bath systems.

Most were used by the ill in treating diseases like rheumatism and TB or utilized as spa services where the well-to-do could take advantage of the exotic Turkish and Russian medicated baths along with massage therapy that was sure to rid anyone of aches and pains. They were luxuriously furnished and well received by anyone in the community who could afford the services. Newfangled equipment was always at hand to rid the patient of any disease.

Like many buildings as they age, this structure fell into disrepair during the mid-1900s. It was used as a home for the disabled and elderly before getting a new lease on life with local shops. The living who entered the sanatorium's doors and those who resided there later still dwell there now in the spirited form—the air echoes with their fear of dying. People taking the walkway outside have heard long, dragged-out moaning. Shadow figures are seen flitting about in the evening. Some who enter feel a sense of doubt press hard on their chest. Then when leaving, an overwhelming relief as if the care provided there left them feeling better.

Left: Tiber Way—Once a sanitorium/spa for the wealthy, after a furniture company and seedy hotel. *Now* the building has been revived and renovated and offers trendy and chic shops.
Tall building to right, Hackett Hotel/The Galley—upscale restaurant and hotel and also haunted.

Old Weiser Building
212 Putnam Street
Marietta, OH 45750
39.415546, -81.454040

Old Casket Maker Ghosts

The Weiser Building (center)—from furniture sales to coffin making to ghosts.

Wieser and Cawley was a traditional furniture store established in 1886 by George Wieser on Front Street. It seems laborers skilled at furniture-making and cabinet-making were also proficient in making caskets, so it was a lucrative side business for woodworkers.

During the mid-twentieth century, it expanded its store to include a funeral home with the help of Dan Cawley, calling themselves the Wieser and Cawley Furniture Store. Furniture was sold on the first, third, and fourth floors, and the funeral chapel was on the second floor. And although during times of recession, folks did not indulge in buying furniture, they always needed a coffin when they died!

So dead people crossed their doors. They have left a part of them inside this building. People catch the tap-tap-tap of footsteps in the building and hear the grind of heavy furniture dragged along the floor.

The Weiser Building

Mid-Ohio Valley Players Theatre
(aka Putnam/The Cinema)
229 Putnam Street
Marietta, OH 45750
39.416253, -81.453903

Theatre of the Dead

The Mid-Ohio Valley Players Theatre opened in 1914 as the Putnam Theatre for vaudeville acts and early movies.

The Mid-Ohio Valley Players Theatre opened in 1914 and was home to vaudeville acts and a movie theatre. It was one of five original theatres located in Marietta and was initially called the Putnam and was later known as The Cinema.

Since 1977, the performing arts tradition has been continued at this beautiful community theatre by the Mid-Ohio Valley Players members who purchased it through a fund drive to raise the money to continue its theatrical tradition. Now the building is alive again with dramas, comedies, musicals, ghost tours, and séance sessions.

The Mid-Ohio Valley Players Theatre and the ticket box. Where a ghostly shadow has been seen by passerby.

Rumor has it that acting is not the only tradition enduring at the Mid-Ohio Valley Players Theatre. It is believed that the ghost of the former owner haunts the structure. He likes to sit in a back row watching the actors readying for performances. He also roams around outside the theatre, keeping an eye out to make sure that all is in working order.

His ghostly presence keeps the show running smoothly for those who watch in the audience. However, behind the sets, another mischievous spirit likes to keep the crews and stagehands on their toes. Because things come up missing right before an act. They vanish, only to reappear at the last moment or even when the show is over.

People's Bank Theatre
(aka Hippodrome/Colony)
222 Putnam Street
Marietta, OH 45750
39.416001, -81.453455

Old Ghosts of an Old Theatre

It has gone through many names since its original format of vaudeville, plays, and silent movies on the corner of Second and Union Street in the early 1900s—

Hippodrome Theatre, New Hippodrome, and Colony Theatre until it has ended up as the People's Bank Theatre. After a fire in 1917, it was razed. The building was brought to life again in 1919, a few blocks away on Putnam Street and with an elegant design, and is now across the street from the Mid-Ohio Valley Players Theatre.

Crowds were eager to watch early vaudeville acts like the family troupe below who would travel from town to town to act in local shows.

I wouldn't be surprised to find that some of the ghostly activity in Marietta's theatres aren't leftover actors still wanting to put on a show!

It featured a giant silver screen, orchestra pit, seven dressing rooms, a chorus girls' room, and a seating capacity of 1,200. During the 1920s, the theatre featured vaudeville acts, magic acts, silent films, and even Broadway plays. By the early 1930s, it boasted "talkies," movies with a soundtrack. During the 1940s, Shea Theatres of New York bought the theatre, renovated it, and renamed the theatre—Colony Cinema. From the 1940s to 1960s, its heyday, it hosted world premiere movies bringing famous actors like Rock Hudson, Judy Garland, and Frank Sinatra into town.

It was restored through fundraising, renovations, and a considerable donation from Peoples Bank, National Association. And those makeovers are what has awakened the ghosts inside this piece of treasured Marietta history. In a Parkersburg News and Sentinel interview by Jasmine Rogers, Tom Moore, co-founder of the Mid-Ohio Valley Ghost Hunters who has led countless tours and ghost hunts, told of hearing the gentle sound of tap shoes in a recording— "It's a definite sound of someone walking right out on the stage with tap shoes," he told the reporter. There is the sound of slamming doors and ghostly footsteps.

A former owner/investor of the theatre lurks in the shadows at the back of the auditorium. He keeps an eye on the rehearsals but also maintains a low profile. Alive, he owned and invested in other show houses but was not one for personal publicity and seldom talked to reporters. And if you care to ask him questions while visiting the theatre, you might want to avoid the subject of politics—he had no interest in political activities.

If you are looking for this man, he was seldom seen by movie-goers or the public except by catching a fleeting glance of the white-haired figure on an opening day of a vaudeville act. He was known to stand inconspicuously near the lobbies of his theatres to make sure his staff treated the patrons respectfully and to make sure the managed theatre was working smoothly. He often visited his theatres, making sure nothing showing was offensive to the public. He would also rebuff young men for smoking near the box office as it annoyed the young women.

The Betsey Mills Club
300 4th Street
Marietta, OH 45750
39.417582, -81.451790

The Practical Skills of Being a Ghost

The Betsey Mills Club—founded by Betsey Mills, a local housewife dedicated to the young women of the community.

In 1911, the Betsey Mills Club was created from a sewing class called the Girls' Monday Club by the wife of First National Bank of Marietta President William Mills. Betsey had started courses in her home and other homes in the community for young women to teach them the practical skills of being a housewife—like sewing and cooking—and provide young women with a sense of camaraderie and kinship. The club grew so popular Betsey purchased a frame house on Fourth Street to accommodate the young women who joined.

After Betsey's death, the original home was upgraded from the frame house to a new brick complex dedicated in 1927 and donated by her husband, William, in memory of his wife's dedication to the community. It still serves its hometown community with childcare services, fitness classes, meeting rooms, and educational programs. There are even second-floor dorm rooms available for women.

So many of the community have come through the doors to enjoy the many services provided. And some have decided to stick around and relish them a little longer. Not only does a mischievous spirit play tricks with the lights in the rooms, making them flicker and dim, but several harmless full-body apparitions come and go around the building. One is a woman caught on video walking a corridor then entering a room where the door was locked solidly. No human hand could have turned that knob and entered! Sometimes clothing disappears for a while, then shows up again without an honest explanation for someone of this earth playing a joke.

So, Betsey Mills is still sticking around along with some of her students. It must not be easy moving onward for some dead, especially if they liked what they were doing when they were alive. Maybe Missus Mills has stuck around to help them on their way, teaching them the practical skills of being a ghost.

George White House
322 Fifth Street
Marietta, OH 45750
39.418911, -81.451841

The White House Ghost

George White House

The house was owned by George White, who made his money in oil near Marietta before becoming governor of Ohio. Since 1954, it has been used by the Alpha Xi Delta sorority. George White haunts the house, knocking things off the walls and opening doors. He protects the girls living within. If a male visitor's intentions are untrue during a visit, he will trip the young man going up the front stairs.

Mound Cemetery
514 Cutler Street
Marietta, OH 45750
39.420377, -81.451900

Ghostly Lights at Mound Cemetery

Mound Cemetery as seen in 1848. Picture: Ancient Monuments of the Mississippi Valley, by E. G. Squier and E. H. Davis

Mound Cemetery in Marietta is a cemetery (circa 1801) built around an ancient Indian burial mound that was part of a more massive complex but is now covered by part of the current town.

Some of those buried in the cemetery date back to Revolutionary War soldiers bestowed land grants for their military services. They include General Rufus Putnam and Benjamin Tupper, the founders of the Ohio Company of Associates.

Mound Cemetery—take a walk around the small cemetery, then take the stairway to the top for a view. Someone once told me they saw the full-bodied apparition of a revolutionary soldier in uniform here kneeling by a grave.

Many enjoy walking the cemetery or strolling the sidewalks just outside. Occasionally, passersby witness tiny lights flickering on the mound and around the gravestones, like that of lightning bugs, but much bigger, small remnants of spirits of Marietta's grand past.

Marietta Castle
418 Fourth Street
Marietta, OH 45750
39.42058,-81.454847

Haunted Castle

The Marietta Castle in 1898. Ralph L. Schroeder, photographer. Image: Washington County Public Library.

The property has a long history of people using its resources. It was first leased around 1808 by Nathaniel Clark and his family for a pottery shop. Around 1855, a home and carriage house were built on the land, and throughout the years of 1808 to 1974, only five families were living on the property-rich families, that is, bankers, oil speculators, and lawyers.

It is enormous and impending, The Castle of Marietta. It is of Gothic Revival style architecture and screams haunted when you peer through the bars of the wrought iron gates. And there is a ghost. It is one of its past owners, Jessie (Davis) Lindsay, who still walks the floors of the building. She was a mere fourteen years old in 1888 when her mother, Lucy Nye Davis, inherited the castle. It was the talk of the town when, eight years later, Jessie married John Lindsay. The reception was held at The Castle. It would be another thirty-three years before the Victorian mansion would become her own home. Jessie lived there alone with a housekeeper and her dog, Suzy, until she died in 1974.

People who have been in the home have seen a woman in historic clothing walking around the building, especially in Jessie's bedroom. They have also seen her peering from inside the windows. There seems to be no guesswork pointing the finger at whose ghost visits The Castle. It is the woman who spent so much of her life there and loved it enough to call it her home until she died.

The Marietta Castle today. Visit it. You might see a ghost!

A few spooky things have happened there. In an interview with Marietta Times in 2016, Kyle Yoho, The Castle's education director said this, "In 1994, a group of volunteers went up in the tower to get a good view of the area and when they came back down the attic door was locked," Yoho told reporter Breckin Wells. "They couldn't get out. They had to yell and scream from the tower until a neighbor heard them to find that the door wasn't even locked."

Jessica Wielitzka, owner of the Hidden Marietta Tour Company, also told of heading to the bathroom near Jessie (Davis) Lindsay's old sitting room. She felt a ghostly slap on her ear, then heard a clear grunt of disapproval.

The Marietta Castle —another historical view. Marietta College Legacy Collection. Harry Philip Fischer Collection

Buckley House
332 Front Street
Marietta, Ohio 45750
39.416393, -81.457456

Ghostly Remnants of Lost Love

The Buckley House is haunted by a young man who committed suicide. *And* perhaps, out of regret and answerability, the narrow minded people who sent him over the edge.

The Buckley House was originally a private residence built for one of the wealthier families of Marietta, the Woodbridges. In the early 1880s, the family sponsored a young man from Guangdong, China, to attend Marietta College to study theology. The plan had been that he would return to his country as a missionary for their church.

Twenty-six-year-old William New Kim, a student at Marietta College, had been converted to Christianity in China and brought over by the Woodbridge family. During his stay, he fell madly in love with a 21-year-old Woodbridge housemaid, Sophia Hoff. She, too, fell in love with the young man.

Knowing their love may not be accepted by those around them, the two were married secretly in practice accepted by his culture, by pledging their love to each other as husband and wife. Not long after, Sophia was sent to Cincinnati to live with her sister and work as a housekeeper there. The couple would remain faithful for some time, sending each other letters of love. However, it was not long before the letters of the two young lovers were found while rifling through his mail, and William New Kim was harshly chastised for living in sin. At the same time, he divulged his secret to his peers, who told him he must choose between his mission work or staying with Sophia. To make matters worse, a letter was sent from Sophia's sister to Kim disapproving of their diverse relationship. Kim became quite distraught, believing he had shamed his family and those who sponsored him. He promised to give up his wife for his vows, but a letter was sent by Sophia mentioning "their darling baby."

He became despondent. Within a few days, he purchased a bottle of chloroform, dressed for burial, and committed suicide in his bed. Such tragedies spurn unrest in spirits. William New Kim's heartbreak and suicide have left their mark on the old Woodbridge home along with the intolerant who judged him so harshly. Although it is an upscale restaurant now, it was once a bed and breakfast stay. During this time and over the years, those staying in the upstairs have heard doors opening and shutting, the sound of footsteps and felt cold spots.

*The Great Flood of 1913
Throughout Marietta Putnam
Bridge for overlook of
Muskingum
Parking if want to walk bridge
Marietta, OH 45750
39.414556, -81.456572*

The Great Flood Ghosts

The flooded Putnam and Front Streets, 1913. Courtesy: Marietta College Legacy Library

Passersby have heard the clip-clop of hooves cantering on the brick streets in Marietta, along with the muffled snorts and whinnies of long-gone horses. Occasionally, a cow's bawling is carried through the air, although fields with cattle are far away from the town. Tourists and locals alike walking through town look up curiously, then dismiss it as a car's tires scraping a curb or dog barking in the distance.

Until cars came along, the main sources of transport in the 1800s were horses, carriages or wagons, and boats, shown here. Floods were brutal to animals when they couldn't find safety. This is the steamboat ED. Roberts pulling a barge on the Ohio River not far from the mouth of the Muskingum. And a horse with a flatbed wagon. Courtesy: Marietta College. Special Collections

These are the ghosts left over from the floods that ravaged this river town along the Ohio River. Because humans, they are not. The residual phantom sounds of rainy days and stormy nights are the carriage horses and farm animals—cows, goats, and mules that were dragged down the river and discarded on the doorsteps of houses after the water receded. Although most people got out alive by finding safety in tall buildings, their animals were not always so lucky.

So, listen on quiet evenings when the rain patters on the streets. You might catch the sound of a ghostly animal left from the floods of the past. And maybe if you are lucky, you will hear one clip-clopping along or hear the faint nicker from one who wants to nuzzle up next to you and be pet.

Anchorage House (aka Putnam Villa/Douglas Putnam House)
498 George Street
Marietta, OH 45750
39.413551, -81.463473

Floating Eliza

The Anchorage or Putnam House (center/rear) in the 1880s.

When Douglas Putnam built this home in the 1850s for his wife, Eliza, it took ten years. The mansion cost an extravagant $65,000, but Eliza had to have it. Eliza fell in love with a friend's home during a visit to New Jersey, and her own Marietta house was modeled after it. It has twenty-two rooms and a tower room with a widow's walk. The Italian villa has sandstone walls quarried from neighboring hills and overlooks the city of Marietta and both the Ohio and Muskingum rivers.

It was initially called 'Putnam Place,' and not until it changed hands later was it deemed 'The Anchorage House.' It hosted many functions for the well-to-do of Marietta.

The Douglas Putnam House in its early days.

Eliza passed away in September of 1862 from heart disease, only three years after the final construction of the home. She was 53 years old. It remained in the family until a couple of years after Douglas died, and his third wife sold it to the Harry Knox family, owners of Knox Boatyard. They renamed it Anchorage. The Anchorage changed hands several times before it became a nursing home for about fifty patients in 1960 and was renamed The Christian Anchorage. By 1984, all the patients had moved to the more modern Marie Antoinette Pavilion right next door.

When it was a nursing home, patients, nurses, and aides would see a shadowy woman on the stairs near the dining room. One nurse also reported seeing a woman in period clothing walking from the stairway to the dining area. And on another occasion, an aide also saw a phantom light wiggling its way across the widow's walk on top. People have seen her both inside the home and outside.

While hiking in the evening at Moonville in Zaleski, I came upon a couple who visited the Anchorage House one afternoon on a self-guided historical tour and were more than happy to tell me their spooky story of the home. They got out of their car after pulling into the graveled side road to the Anchorage. Just as the woman turned to head toward the building, she stopped in utter horror. Not a stone's throw away was a full-bodied apparition of a woman floating several feet above the grassy lawn!

The Washington County Historical Society now owns the property. Hidden Marietta guides and paranormal investigators provide haunted history tours. Today, Eliza pops up occasionally to surprise those visiting this historic site. You may see her shadow while she peers out of one of the windows or walks the hallways and stairways. Voices also resonate in the building, and shadow figures prowl the many rooms. Those who have attended ghostly tours have had their hair tugged and touched. And if you are lucky (or unlucky depending upon your views of supernatural surprises), you might see a spooky dead woman floating around the yard.

The Anchorage House today. Historical. Ghostly.

Harmar Tavern
205 Maple Street
Marietta, OH 45750
39.411637, -81.460039

Brews and Boos—Old Woman in a Black Dress at the Harmar Tavern

Fort Harmar—a part of Marietta's past.

On the western bank of the mouth of the Muskingum River, Colonel Josiah Harmar gave orders to build a fort. The objective was to prevent settlers from squatting on the territory per treaties with the Indians. By the 1790s, the fort was abandoned, and Marietta eventually expanded across the river to it.

One of those buildings in the historic neighborhood of Harmar is the Harmar Tavern, which has been in business since 1900. Strange things happen in the tavern. Chairs move to appear as if patrons are sitting in them. Lights flicker. And then, there's the older woman seen in the back of the room. She is dressed in dark clothing and blends quite well with the shadows. Who she is, no one knows. One must wonder if she is a wandering spirit, a devout church-goer leftover from Prohibition who regards those imbibing in the brew there as heathens, scamps, and scoundrels.

Harmar Tavern. Home to brews and ghosts.

Fort Harmar Monument
409 Fort Street
Marietta, OH 45750
39.409859, -81.457675

A Front-Row Seat to the Wreck of
Stern-wheeler Washington

EXPLOSION OF THE WASHINGTON, 1816.

The Washington —exploded at Point Harmar in 1816. *Photo: Lloyd's steamboat directory, and disasters ...Lloyd, James T.*

The Washington was launched in 1816 out of Wheeling, West Virginia. It was something of a unique and sensational affair—a stern-wheeler with her paddlewheel located at her stern rather than mounted on either side.

She also had a single stack instead of the double stack noted on most riverboats of her time. She was even well-appointed with private rooms and a bar. And she had an accomplished captain as Henry Shreve and a well-trained crew. What she did not have, however, was good luck.

A stern-wheeler much like the ill-fated Washington.
Image: Historical River Highway of the Northwest

Although not her maiden voyage, the steamboat was somewhat on her training drive. When she arrived at Marietta, there were no passengers on board between June 6 and 7. There she stayed anchored safely at the wharf so curious onlookers could get a view and walk a gangplank to peek inside—there were not many steamboats on the edge of the west then—maybe only a few. She then made her way past the Muskingum to safely anchor off Point Harmar on Saturday, June 8, where she remained another night.

On Sunday morning of June 9, the crew readied themselves to make their way up the river. The engine room crew lighted her fires, and they waited for steam pressure to build. Once the steam was up, the whistle blasted out, and workers released ropes from the pier.

She eased out into the flow of water, and all should have been well except for one slight problem—she had no power as the throttle was yet to be opened.

Suddenly, the current of the Ohio River caught the boat, shooting it outward. At the same time, she was also getting swept by another current from the mouth of the Muskingum, which turned her awkwardly. She was swept uncontrolled over toward the Virginia side of the river. The captain, noting with horror that the boat was at the mercy of the rivers as the vessel had no power, shouted for an anchor to be set into the water and a second to be on hand in case the boat kept moving. This particular anchor, called a kedge anchor, would be used to reposition the stern-wheeler in the proper direction by pulling it into position—especially under the dire circumstances the boat was in now. It needed as many men as possible on the stern that could be available to do just that, and the captain ordered nearly everyone aboard to drag in the rope, pulling it across the river.

Marietta (right forefront) and just beyond is the Muskingum River, followed by Harmar (right rear) where the boat was safely anchored until June 9th. Where the sternwheeler is in the image is where the trouble began—

Standing on Harmar Point where the boat was pulled by the two rivers and where the captain must have realized, with horror, the boat had no power. Image taken just below Fort Harmar monument— 409 Fort Street, Marietta, OH 45750 (39.409859, -81.457675)

What they did not know was that they were standing right over a boiler with a defective safety valve. And it was going to explode. It did burst, the cylinder, and scalding water heaved upward, knocking some of the men, including the captain, completely off the boat. Others were entirely skinned to the bone, while some were burned and tried desperately to peel off their clothing, only have their flesh come with it. Mangled men were scattered on the deck. Pieces of shrapnel from the blast had taken whole arms and legs with them, leaving body parts scattered on the boat. Some men had their eyes burned out of the sockets while others' faces were indistinguishable. Others had breathed in the scalding steam which burned their lungs. All who went into the water were pulled from its depths except one young man named Joseph whose body was swept downstream.

Seven were killed instantly. Five more would die over the next few days; their screams and sobs of agony were heard along the shore and far into town.

It was said the horror among the crowd who had, in alarm, run to the water's edge after the explosion was unspeakable. They were powerless to do little more than watch helplessly and listen.

Celeron Monument

If you were standing here and near the Celeron Monument (monument showing where a lead tablet was placed at the mouth of the Muskingum River in the 1750s left by a French explorer claiming the area) in 1816, you would have had a front-row seat to the explosion. Now you might see ghosts leftover from the horrible ordeal. Celeron Monument—100-106 Gilman Avenue, Marietta, OH 45750 (39.407586, -81.459924)

The Washington was repaired and rechristened months later. She had a long, sound life after that. A new crew was hired, and the explosion was rarely brought to attention except to say it was the first one in the west. But on warm nights when the water is rolling along the Ohio River, stop and listen along the bank. If you were standing here on June 9, 1816, you would have a front-row seat to the horrific disaster. Today, though, you can hear the rush of water catch an occasional shout from one boater to another. But you may also hear the ghostly sounds of an old steamboat's past—the cries of those men who died on that fateful day because it is said, such horrific moments stick to time and places. And they never go away.

Harmar Bridge
Marietta Harbor Bridge
Marietta, OH 45750
39.412132, -81.455390

Shadow on the Harmar Bridge

Harmar Bridge where I heard a ghostly story.

You can walk this old railroad trestle across to Harmar. You can get a good vantage point for a view of the Muskingum River as it heads into the Ohio River. It was a wooden covered bridge in 1856 open for both pedestrians and wagons and used often. Once the Marietta and Pittsburgh Railway was completed in the early 1870s in the city, it was strengthened to accept trains. Now it is open to foot traffic. If you dare—

I walked it last winter during a frigid 20-degree day to get a shot of the river. Before I did, I hesitated for a moment because it was freezing outside, and the walkway was ice-covered. I had to work up to it. The wind was blasting, and my toes were frozen. I was not even sure that I still had a nose on my face because I thought surely it had frozen solid and fallen off a block over on my walk to get there.

Two women had stopped and were peering at the walking bridge with uncertainty. I figured they had traversed it once today and were wondering if they wanted to risk their lives and tread across the slippery walkway again. So, I asked them if they had crossed, and was it too ice-slick to walk? I figured that was the reason for their hesitation.

They just shook their heads then laughed softly. It seems during another visit, one of the two had walked it at night when the moon was lighting the sky. A shadow had accompanied her, and while she peered over her shoulder, she swore it was not her own. Three times, when she stopped, it also stopped. However, it paused a little too late and almost crossed over her shadow. With heart pumping, she could not decide if she imagined the stalker silhouette or if it was her eyes playing tricks on her. What seemed an eternity passed while she continued quick steps. Then she decided to assess her sanity one last time. At the fourth and final time, she paused her steps. She could stand it no longer and sprinted back to the side she had come. It seems the shadow, this time, had passed her own and had continued onward towards Harmar!

Beverly Lock
Ohio Street
Beverly, OH 45715
39.546197,-81.642129

Tragedy at Beverly Lock

A lone steamboat making a ghostly passage along the Muskingum River. The Buckeye Belle would take this trek along these waters one last time in 1852 before leaving ghosts in its wake. *Picture: Marietta College, Legacy Library.*

What could be more intriguing than stories of ghosts along the river lingering around a lock where a riverboat explosion happened almost 170 years ago? Only twenty miles from Marietta, the Buckeye Belle made one last fateful journey before becoming one of the most horrific disasters in Ohio history.

The real story begins on November 12th of 1852, as the Buckeye Belle riverboat made its way along the Muskingum River at Beverly, Ohio. It had forty passengers and was a favorite boat to travel along the river. In addition, it was on a usual mail route along the northwestern turnpike to Zanesville.

The Steamboat S.R. Van Metre made trips along the Ohio River near Marietta just like the Buckeye Belle worked along the Muskingum. *Picture: Marietta College, Legacy Library.*

The boat had just made it to the guard lock when suddenly, a thundering explosion tore through the air. The boilers had been completely blown to pieces—overheating with too much steam and too little water. The most sizable portion was hurled more than fifty yards over the boat and down the canal. A second piece was lobbed to the guard lock, while a third was flung and alit near the top of the hill some three or four hundred yards from the wreck. There were bricks found as far away as the top of the highest elevation above the town. The boat was torn asunder.

The November 25th Gallipolis Journal stated the following about the catastrophe: *Even the lower deck and hull are so completely torn to fragments that there hardly remains whole plank forward of the wheel house, and the cabin, pilot house and every thing back of the wheel house shivered to atoms, and strewn to the four winds, covering the ground and water for a great distance around with kindling wood furniture, trunks and baggage, limb and bodies of men, in the most awful manner that the imagination could possibly conceive. . . There were about 40 passengers on board, (besides the boat's crew,) among whom were seven or eight ladies from this town—* There were twenty-four people killed, and eyewitnesses stated there were mutilated corpses up and down the river. Some bodies were never recovered. On foggy, rainy November evenings, if you listen hard along the river at the lock, you can hear the sounds of the men working on the riverboat that fateful autumn day back in 1852. There have been stories of ghostly riverboat whistles and voices heard, but the source of the sounds never found. It does not have to be evening or foggy to get a strange feeling there.

Me, standing at the Beverly Lock. It gives off an eerie aura even with the pretty town nearby.

Citations for Stories:

Lafayette:
—History — Historic Lafayette Hotel. (n.d.). Retrieved from http://www.lafayettehotel.com/history
—History, mystery and hauntings surround Marietta. (n.d.). Retrieved from https://www.newsandsentinel.com/news/local-news/2013/10/history-mystery-and-hauntings-surround-marietta/
—Gary L. Bergstrand, Hocking College Professor

The Levee House:
—The Levee House // Marietta, OH. (n.d.). Retrieved from https://www.theleveehousemarietta.com/
The long history and many lives of Marietta's Levee'House. (n.d.). Retrieved from https://www.newsandsentinel.com/news/community-news/2019/02/the-long-history-and-many-lives-of-mariettas-levee%E2%80%88house/
—History of Washington County, Ohio: With Illustrations and Biographical Sketches. (1881).
—Memory and Masonry: A History of the Levee House. (2018, July 31). Retrieved from https://clutchmov.com/memory-and-masonry-a-history-of-the-levee-house/
—Sturtevant, L. (2010). Haunted Marietta: History and Mystery in Ohio's Oldest City. Charleston, SC: Arcadia Publishing.
—Williams, H. (1881). Page 365. In History of Washington County, Ohio, with illustrations and biographical sketches.

People's Bank Theatre:
—Ghostly Apparitions, Voices Remain at Historic Ohio Theatre. (n.d.). Retrieved from https://www.phantomsandmonsters.com/2010/06/ghostly-apparitions-voices-remain-at.html
—Peoples Bank Theatre. (n.d.). Retrieved from http://cinematreasures.org/theaters/1653
——History. (2015, October 10). Retrieved from https://peoplesbanktheatre.com/about/history/
—Bancorp, P. (2013, February 27). Historic Hippodrome-Colony Theatre Renamed Peoples Bank Theatre. Retrieved from https://www.prnewswire.com/news-releases/historic-hippodrome-colony-theatre-renamed-peoples-bank-theatre-193584101.html
—Rogers, Jasmine Interview of Tom Moore. (n.d.). History, mystery and hauntings surround Marietta. Retrieved from https://www.newsandsentinel.com/news/local-news/2013/10/history-mystery-and-hauntings-surround-marietta/
—https://digitalcommons.buffalostate.edu/cgi/viewcontent.cgi?article=1002&context=msheascrapbooks

The Anchorage:
—https://www.wchshistory.org/anchorage-history
—The_Times_Recorder October 31, 1992 Mystery Cloaks 18th Century Mansion in Marietta Cartmell, Connie

Marietta Castle:
—https://www.academia.edu/33106928/Preliminary_Notes_on_Early_Nineteenth_Century_Pottery_Production_in_Southeastern_Ohio
—Marietta Castle – Marietta, OH | American Ghost Stories. https://americanghoststories.com/mid-west-ghost-stories/ohio/marietta-castle-marietta
—Castle ghost tour Friday | News, Sports, Jobs - Marietta Times. https://www.mariettatimes.com/news/local-news/2016/10/castle-ghost-tour-friday/

—Washington County Ohio - Haunting and Ghosts - Anchorage ....
https://www.hauntedhocking.com/
Haunted_Ohio_Washington_County.htm
Hackett Hotel/Tiber Way:
—https://www.mariettatimes.com/news/local-news/2014/11/2-old-gems/
—Marietta Daily Leader 1 Nov 1899, Page 3
—Marietta Daily Leader 16 Jan 1900, Page 3
—Marietta Daily Leader April 12, 1900
—The Galley Restaurant and Hackett Hotel. (n.d.). Retrieved from http://theresashauntedhistoryofthetri-state.blogspot.com/2014/03/the-galley-restaurant-and-hackett-hotel.html
—Sturtevant, L. (2010). Haunted Marietta: History and Mystery in Ohio's Oldest City. Charleston, SC: Arcadia Publishing.
—Top 8 Most Haunted Hotels in Ohio (Updated 2019). (n.d.). Retrieved from https://www.hauntedrooms.com/8-haunted-hotels-in-ohio
—hiddenmarietta.com
Buckley House:
—Year: 1870; Census Place: Marietta Ward 2, Washington, Ohio; Roll: M593_1279; Page: 332B; Image: 159; Family History Library Film: 552778
—Catalog: 1946- Marietta College Bulletin, Marietta College. Publ 1879
—Racer, Theresa. The Buckley House's
—Bismarck Tribune, Bismarck ND November 11, 1881
—Cincinnati Enquirer. Nov9, 1881 New Kim Shuffles Off at Marietta
Fort Harmar:
—Wielitzka, J. (2017, December 29). Marietta's Haunted Hotels & Restaurants. Retrieved from https://www.hiddenmarietta.com/single-post/2017/12/29/Mariettas-Haunted-Hotels-Restaurants
—Fort Harmar | Marietta | Ohio. (n.d.). Retrieved from http://touringohio.com/history/fort-harmar.html
Buckley Island:
—Ohio River Islands National Wildlife Refuge
—Wilmington News Journal August 9, 1921
—Delphos Daily April 9, 1930
—The Daily Times June 22, 1964
—Smallpox, pioneer scourge. (n.d.). Retrieved from http://earlymarietta.blogspot.com/2019/10/smallpox-pioneer-scourge.html
—The Marietta, Times, January 20, 2010
— The Marietta Register, June 30, 1898
—Harmar Village - Marietta, Ohio. (n.d.). Retrieved from https://www.facebook.com/www.HarmarVillageMariettaOhio/posts/2676933345713334?comment_id=2677127229027279&comment_tracking=%7B%22tn%22%3A%22R%22%7D
Weiser Building:
—Sturtevant, L. (2010). Haunted Marietta: History and Mystery in Ohio's Oldest City. Charleston, SC: Arcadia Publishing.
—https://www.flickr.com/photos/25229906@N00/41738239644
St Cloud:
—The Baltimore Sun March 26, 1898
—https://www.sandandorsnow.com/2017/04/haunted-history-of-marietta-ohio-7-tales/
—Marietta Daily Leader Wednesday March 30, 1898 Unluckiest of All George Hudson Meets His Death in a Shocking Manner
Harmar Bridge:
—Putnam St Bridge Replacement Across the Muskingum River, City of Marietta, Washington County: Environmental Impact Statement. (1996).

Harmar Tavern:
—https://www.hiddenmarietta.com/
Betsey Mills:
—https://www.ohiomagazine.com/ohio-life/article/haunted-history-4-ohio-ghost-tours
—Sturtevant, L. (2010). Haunted Marietta: History and Mystery in Ohio's Oldest City. Charleston, SC: Arcadia Publishing.
The Washington:
—https://disasteroushistory.blogspot.com/2016/09/the-steamboats-washington-enterprise.html
—Virginia Argus June 15, 1816 Particulars of a Late Dreadful Accident
—http://www.gendisasters.com/ohio/14763/harmar-oh-steamboat-washington-explosion-jun-1816
—Lloyd, J. T. (1856). Lloyd's Steamboat Directory, and Disasters on the Western Waters: Containing the History of the First Application of Steam, as a Motive Power; the Lives of John Fitch and Robert Fulton ... History of the Early Steamboat Navigation on Western Waters ... a Complete List of Steamboats and All Other Vessels Now Afloat on the Western Rivers and Lakes ... Maps of the Ohio and Mississippi Rivers ... History of All the Rail Roads in the United States ... One Hundred Fine Engravings, and Sixty Maps ..
Beverly Lock:
—Beverly, OH Steamer BUCKEYE BELLE Explosion, Nov 1852 .... http://www.gendisasters.com/ohio/6296/beverly-oh-steamer-buckeye-belle-explosion-nov-1852
—Daily chronicle & sentinel. (Augusta, Ga.) 1837-1876 .... https://gahistoricnewspapers.galileo.usg.edu/lccn/sn82015215/1852-11-25/ed-1/seq-2/
—Washington County Ohio - Haunting and Ghosts - Anchorage .... https://www.hauntedhocking.com/Haunted_Ohio_Washington_County.htm

Walking Map of Ghost Stories

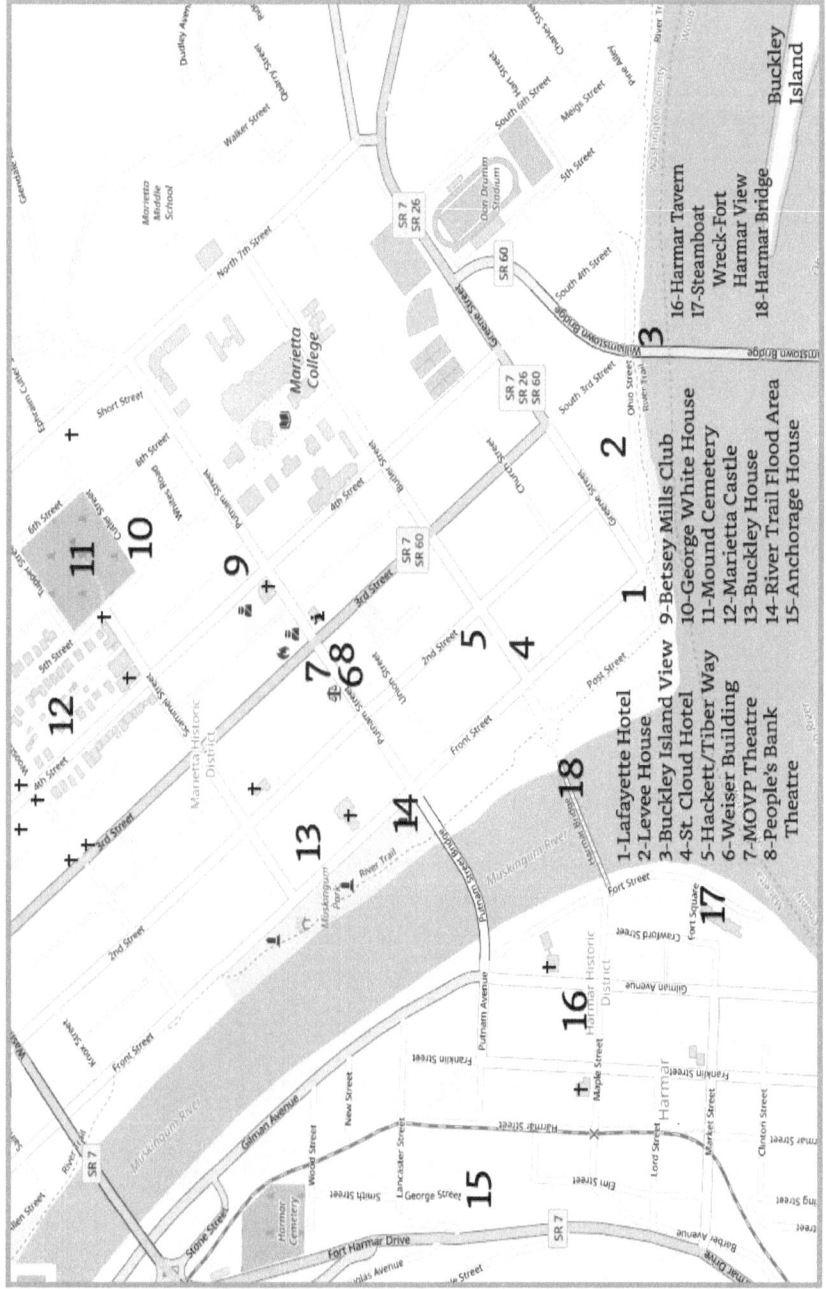

1-Lafayette Hotel
2-Levee House
3-Buckley Island View
4-St. Cloud Hotel
5-Hackett/Tiber Way
6-Weiser Building
7-MOVP Theatre
8-People's Bank Theatre
9-Betsey Mills Club
10-George White House
11-Mound Cemetery
12-Marietta Castle
13-Buckley House
14-River Trail Flood Area
15-Anchorage House
16-Harmar Tavern
17-Steamboat Wreck-Fort Harmar View
18-Harmar Bridge

www.ingramcontent.com/pod-product-compliance
Lightning Source LLC
Chambersburg PA
CBHW051309250626
47155CB00009B/3502